Licensed exclusively to Top That Publishing Ltd
Tide Mill Way, Woodbridge, Suffolk, IP12 1AP, UK
www.topthatpublishing.com
Copyright © 2016 Emma Levey
All rights reserved
0 2 4 6 8 9 7 5 3 1
Manufactured in China

Written and illustrated by Emma Levey

ISBN 978-1-78445-658-0

A catalogue record for this book is available from the British Library

'For my family and special thanks to Dan, Lucy and Greg'

Hattie Peck
The Journey Home

Written and illustrated
by Emma Levey

Hattie Peck
loved eggs.

What she loved even more
was what hatched out of them ...

Her
family!

Hattie had braved the elements rescuing abandoned eggs around the world.

Big ones,

small ones,

no matter what their size,
she loved each hatchling
just the same.

Life was different now that
Hattie's home was full ...

Outings were chaotic,

mealtimes were busy,

bathtimes were wet,

and bedtimes were...

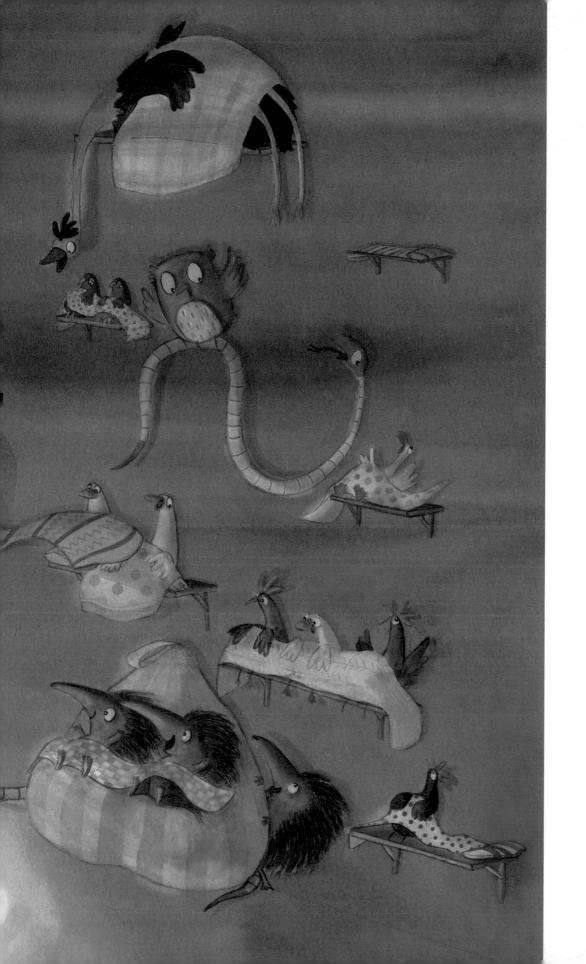

... well,
a bit of a
nightmare!

But Hattie Peck didn't
mind. She was happy.

Despite the chaos,
Hattie's family shared
many happy moments.

Their big days out,

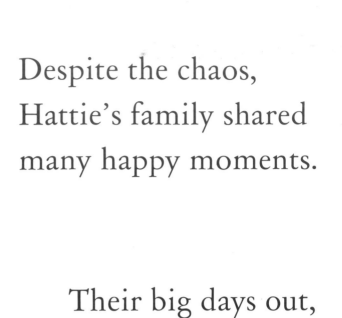

and their
cosy, twinkling
Christmases.

But what they **all** loved most, was their birthday...

because every year,
Hattie made each hatchling
a perfectly-knitted treat,

just for them.

'I love it!'

But Hattie knew
the time was near
for her family to
embark on a
new adventure.

The hatchlings were all grown up.
It was time for them to fly the nest.

Bags got packed,
and snacks were prepared.

With a nervous flutter, they left the coop.

Hattie and her hatchlings
travelled across stormy seas.

'What enormous waves!' Hattie cried. 'Hold on tight!'

And then began
the many goodbyes.

They ran across rooftops,

'Goodbye!'

'Farewell!'

hopped over chimneys,

'So long!'

and slid down gutters.

Soaring over gigantic cities, Hattie gently guided her precious little hatchlings.

She tried not to
look down ...

heights made
Hattie shudder!

Hattie's family was getting smaller and smaller ...
but their journey was getting
bigger and **bigger!**

They hauled themselves up mountains,

and teetered across treacherous ledges!

They crept through gloomy,
dark caves, deep down
below the ground.

The last of Hattie's hatchlings battled blustery winds,

pouring rain and heavy snow.

Until it was just Hattie and a long journey home ...

alone.

Hattie imagined her hatchlings
busy living their lives and
it made her happy.

But now it was their birthday, the first one apart,
and Hattie couldn't help wishing they were ...

'Surprise!' they all shouted.

'We've made something for you,' they said.

'Wow!' Hattie cried.
'A perfectly-knitted treat,

just for me!

I love it. But what I love
the most, is my family.'